RISE OF THE
RABBITS

BARRY HUTCHISON

What do other readers think?

Here are some comments left on the Fiction Express
blog about this book:

*"This story is so funny!!! You completely change
the perception of these cute little bunny rabbits into
horrible little maniacs."*
Grace, student blogger, Bedfordshire

*"Rise of the Rabbits is the most amazing book on
Fiction Express by far!! I can't believe you've turned
a cute little bunny wabbit into something paranormal!!
LOL! I love it and it's amazing!"*
Melissa R, student blogger, Lancaster

*"Ok so I've heard of cats planning to rule the earth
and rats and pigs even chinchillas' but BUNNIES are
completely unheard of. It's a really original and funny idea."*
HGW2, student blogger, Hampshire

"This book was amazing!"
Alpesh, student blogger, Leicester

Contents

Chapter 1

Rabbit on the Loose

The day the school rabbit tried to kill everyone started out pretty much like any other.

I woke up early, like I always do. My twin brother, Harvey, finally dragged himself out of bed at half past eight as usual. Mum says if sleeping ever became an Olympic sport, Harvey and my dad would compete for gold every time.

Mind you, at least Dad does something useful when he's awake. He's a botanist, which means he travels the world finding and collecting rare plants.

Harvey, on the other hand, doesn't do anything for anybody. He's either up in his room playing Minecraft or downstairs watching Minecraft videos on the laptop. Or he's finding new ways to be as annoying as humanly possible. Usually to me.

And then there's my mum. My mum is... well, she's kind of Supermum. I get up at 7 am every day, but Mum has already been up, taken our dog, Scraps, for a walk and started breakfast in that time.

Anyway, I should introduce myself. I'm Lola. I love swimming, archery and football, hate Minecraft (seriously, what's the point?), and when I'm older want to be either a top athlete, the prime minister… or maybe to win *The X-Factor*.

I *did* want to be a vet, but that was before what happened with the school rabbit, Mr Lugs…. But I'm getting ahead of myself.

Like I said, it all started normally enough. Harvey and I went to school (I like it, he hates it), had lunch in the canteen (I hate it, he loves it), then were picked to take Mr Lugs home for the weekend (we both liked that).

Dad was asleep on the armchair in the living room when we got home. He'd arrived back from a trip to some jungle or other the day before, so he kept nodding off because of the jetlag. Well, that was his excuse, anyway.

Harvey thought it would be funny to put Mr Lugs on Dad's lap while he was asleep, to see what would happen when he woke up. For once, I agreed with him, so I gently set the rabbit down on my dad's outstretched legs, then tiptoed away.

"This is going to be brilliant!" Harvey whispered. He took out his mobile phone and started recording. We half-crouched behind the couch and waited.

And waited.

And waited.

"Dad's a really deep sleeper, isn't he?" I said.

Mr Lugs was wriggling about on Dad's lap, his little nose twitching away like it always does. He's quite heavy for a rabbit, because the kids in school are always feeding him treats, but Dad still didn't notice.

"This is taking ages," Harvey grumbled. He cupped a hand to the side of his mouth and shouted, "DAD!"

Dad jolted awake. He looked down, saw Mr Lugs, then let out an ear-splitting scream. In one swift movement he leaped out of the seat, catapulting Mr Lugs across the room.

End over end the poor bunny flipped, twirling and spinning, his fluffy white fur making him look like a tiny cloud.

Jumping up from behind the couch I dived, arms reaching like a goalkeeper. Everything seemed to go into slow motion as I sailed through the air, hands together, fingers outstretched.

I saw Harvey turn his phone camera towards me. I heard Dad give a little gasp of shock. And I saw the look of pure terror on Mr Lugs's little face as he rocketed helplessly across the room.

I'm not going to make it, I thought, but then my fingertips felt something furry and my hands wrapped firmly around the tumbling bunny's body.

I landed with a *thud* on the carpet, almost winding myself. But it didn't matter. I had done it! I had saved Mr Lugs! Mr Lugs looked at me, and I'm pretty sure he smiled. Well, maybe not smiled, but he definitely blinked.

"Whoa," said Harvey, tapping the screen of his phone, "that's *totally* going on YouTube!"

Dad was pretty impressed with the catch, but not so impressed by us putting a rabbit on him when he was asleep. He started going on about how the school shouldn't have sent Mr Lugs home with us, and about how it'd wind up the dog, and blah-de-blah-de-blah.

Luckily he sat down mid-rant, and almost immediately fell back to sleep. Mum was out walking Scraps, so Harvey and I decided we'd take it in turns to look after Mr Lugs. I wanted to go first, but Harvey insisted he do it.

I didn't bother arguing. I knew he'd get bored quickly, then I'd have Mr Lugs to myself for the rest of the evening. I went upstairs to get changed, then came back down to find Harvey in the living room, hunched over the laptop.

"That video has already had twenty hits!" he told me as soon as I entered the room. "It's practically gone viral!"

"Right," I said, not interested. I looked around. "Where's Mr Lugs?"

"What?" Harvey said, frowning. "He's... I dunno. He's around."

"Around where?" I demanded. "Because he's not around here."

Harvey shrugged. "Kitchen, maybe?"

I sighed. I knew Harvey would get bored quickly, but this was a record even for him. I headed through to the kitchen.

As I pushed open the door, a cool breeze fluttered around my face.

"Oh no," I gasped. The back door was wide open! I dashed out into the garden, eyes darting across the gravel and grass. "Mr Lugs!" I called. "Mr Lugs where are you?"

And that was when I saw it....

That was when I saw the door of the greenhouse.

My dad has three huge greenhouses in the garden, where he keeps the plants and flowers from his travels. He has stickers on the doors to colour-code them – green is for common plants found all over the place and orange is for rare or endangered species.

The final greenhouse has a red sticker and is the biggest of all. That's where Dad keeps the ultra-rare and unusual stuff – the plants and flowers no one else has ever discovered. Harvey and I aren't even allowed to set foot in the place.

And now the door was open.

Chapter 2

Monster Munch!

With a glance back into the house,
I rushed to the red greenhouse. A wave
of weird smells wafted out from within.
The greenhouse was heated to keep the
plants alive, and I felt beads of sweat
forming on my forehead as soon as I
stepped inside.

"Mr Lugs?" I whispered. "Mr Lugs,
are you here?"

The flowers in the greenhouse
were all the colours of the rainbow.
I would have loved to stop and

look at them, but there was no time. If Dad caught me I'd be in big trouble.

I searched around quickly, but there was no sign of Mr Lugs anywhere. I'd just about decided he wasn't in there when I heard something that made my blood run cold.

Nibbling.

Something was nibbling Dad's exotic flowers!

I hurried in the direction of the sound, dodging down a narrow alleyway of plants, and taking a left at a blue bush with purple flowers.

The nibbling was noisier now. I thought it was because I was getting closer, but then I realized it wasn't just that it was getting louder, it was getting faster, too. The soft nibbling had become a frantic, frenzied munching.

Suddenly, a flower over on my right vanished. A second later, another one disappeared – yanked down out of sight behind a table.

A third flower went the same way, then a fourth, then a fifth! I heard a scurrying and scrabbling on the dirt floor. One of the tables rose up, bumped by something racing below it. There was a *crash* as a small tree came toppling down, smashing a pane of glass.

Half-eaten leaves and bits of twig were tossed up into the air as the tree was torn to pieces by the *something* that was in there with me.

Holding my breath, I backed slowly towards the door, not wanting to stay a moment longer. I had almost made it when my heel caught on a bag of compost. My arms flailed wildly, I let out a yelp, then I toppled backwards to the ground.

The gnawing sound stopped. I peered through a gap in the plants and table legs, and I saw something terrifying. It was the size of a large dog, with mean, green eyes that stared out from a mass of dirty white fur. The monster's two front teeth looked razor-sharp.

It was only when it twitched its nose that I realized the terrible truth.

It was Mr Lugs, the school rabbit.

Only he wasn't exactly a rabbit any more.

Chapter 3

The Fast and the Furry-ous

Five minutes ago, Mr Lugs had been one of the cutest, cuddliest little creatures I had ever seen. None of those words described what was now staring at me through the gaps in Dad's exotic plants.

If you closed one eye and really tried, you could maybe imagine that he still looked rabbit-shaped. He still had his long ears, and his fluffy paws… but his ears were now almost a metre in length, and each paw was as big as a boxer's fist.

What really terrified me was the look in his eyes. When we'd brought Mr Lugs home from school he'd had a sort of blank bunny stare, even when Dad had accidentally launched him across the room at high speed.

Now, though, his eyes looked intelligent. Worse than that, they looked mean. And even worse still, they looked *hungry*!

I could tell from his expression that Mr Lugs hadn't just grown big, he'd grown nasty. He was no longer the loveable ball of fur the teacher called her "little fluffy-wuffy", he was something dangerous. And he had me in his sights.

I glanced at the door to the greenhouse. It was only nine or ten steps away. If I could get to my feet and make a run for it I might be able to escape before Mr Lugs could catch me.

But what then? Could I reach the house in time, or would he come bounding on to my back before I got there? How fast could mutant bunny rabbits run? I had absolutely no idea, but I had a horrible feeling the answer was "faster than me".

A jolt of shock shook me as I peered back through the gap in the plants. Mr Lugs was nowhere to be seen!

My eyes darted left, right, up, down, searching frantically for any sign of–

There!

From the corner of my eye I saw a mound of white fur come creeping between the table legs towards me.

There was no time to get up, no time to run, no time to do anything.

So that's exactly what I did: nothing. I remembered reading somewhere about people pretending to be dead to avoid being attacked by wild animals. Well, Mr Lugs was the wildest-looking animal I'd ever seen. It had to be worth a try.

I let my head drop and my muscles relax. Closing my eyes, I held my breath as Mr Lugs padded… steadily… closer.

I almost screamed when I felt his huge nose snuffle at my feet, but somehow managed to stop myself. My heart was pounding in my chest. I was sure he would hear it – his ears were certainly big enough – and work out that I was faking. Any moment, I expected the sharp sting of his teeth snapping down on me.

His long whiskers brushed across my face, tickling my nose with their tips. *Don't sneeze,* I told myself. *Don't you dare sneeze!*

But it was no use. I could already feel the sneeze building. Any second now a full-scale nose trembler was going to erupt! Any second after that, I would be rabbit food.

A-A-ATCHOO!

The force of the sneeze made me sit up sharply. I opened my eyes, expecting to see the gaping mouth of Mr Lugs come lunging towards my head.

But I didn't see Mr Lugs's mouth. I didn't see any of him, in fact. The rabbit had hopped it. Mr Lugs was gone.

I sat there for almost a minute, frozen in terror. My brain tried to talk my legs into moving, but my legs were having none of it, insisting they were perfectly happy where they were, *thank you very much.*

Finally, with a lot of effort, I forced my feet to do as they were told. Shakily, I stood up, crept out of the greenhouse and peered around the garden.

There was no sign of Mr Lugs over by the other two greenhouses. He didn't seem to be near the shed, either, and the bin wasn't big enough for him to hide behind.

From the house there came a soft *creak* as the kitchen door swung gently on its hinges, or, to be precise, on one hinge.

I raced towards it, suddenly no longer afraid for myself but for –

"Dad!"

Clattering into the kitchen, I skidded to a stop. The table and chairs had been knocked over, and there was a huge dent in the fridge.

The door leading through to the hall was still closed, but there was a massive rabbit-shaped hole in the wall right beside it. Mr Lugs must have rocketed straight through the plaster at high speed.

I ducked hurriedly through the hole and scrambled across the hall. The living room door was hanging from one hinge, and even as I called out Dad's name again, a part of me knew I wasn't going to get an answer.

The living room was a mess. The lamp was toppled, the coffee table was on its side and the TV was lying face down on the carpet. The armchair Dad had been sitting on was a twisted skeleton of stuffing and springs.

And my dad, as I'd feared, was nowhere to be seen.

The front window had been smashed and a gust of cool wind blew the curtains back and forth. I ran to it and peered out at the front garden. There were two sets of holes in the grass that I knew must have been made by Mr Lugs as he bounded across the garden, but the footprints were huge. Could he still be growing?!

From upstairs, I heard a low groan. "Harvey!" I gasped.

Scurrying quietly to the bottom of the staircase, I listened. More groans. Low and miserable, like someone in pain.

I searched around for a weapon, but all I could find was my dad's golf umbrella. I picked it up and tried swishing it from side to side. It would have to do.

Slowly, softly, step by step I tiptoed up the stairs. The closer I got to Harvey's room, the louder the groaning became. There was another sound, too – a sort of hissing noise like an angry cat might make.

Or an angry rabbit?

Chapter 4

A Hole Lot of Trouble

I kicked open the door and leapt into the room. Waggling the umbrella in front of me like a sword, I screamed, "Get away from him you big-eared freak!" at the top of my voice.

Harvey looked up from his computer and blinked. "Who are you calling a big-eared freak?" he asked, touching his ears to make sure they hadn't grown unexpectedly.

"What was that groaning?" I demanded.

"Zombies," said Harvey.

I leaned on the door frame to support myself. "Zombies?" I spluttered. This day was going from bad to worse.

"Yeah. In Minecraft," Harvey said, pointing to his computer monitor.

A loud *hissssss* echoed around the room. "Well what's that?" I asked.

"Creepers! They're going to–"

KA-BLOOOM!

Harvey stared at the screen. For a moment, it looked as if he was about to cry. "Great. They've destroyed my house," he said. "That was your fault."

"Forget Minecraft!" I cried, grabbing Harvey by the arm. "Mr Lugs has mutated into a giant evil bunny-monster. He's taken Dad!"

Harvey's face went pale. "You can't be serious!" he gasped. "*Forget Minecraft?*

Do you have any idea how.... Wait. What did you say about a giant evil bunny-monster?"

I dragged Harvey out of his chair. "No time to explain," I said, pulling him on to the landing. I bounded down the stairs three at a time, Harvey stumbling along behind me.

Throwing open the front door, we raced out into the garden, along the path and on to the street. In the distance, I could see a row of crushed cars, their alarms all going off together. It was hard to tell over the screeching din, but for a moment I thought I heard screaming, too.

"What's going on?" Harvey asked. "Why's the front window broken? Why is there white stuff in your hair?"

"It's plaster from the hole in the kitchen wall," I explained. "The house is trashed, Dad is missing. Didn't you hear any of that happening?"

Harvey shook his head. "I was fighting the Ender Dragon…
in *Minecraft*!" he added slowly as if I was completely stupid. "Hey, there's Mum!"

I spun on the spot. *Mum*! There she was, striding along with Scraps at her heels. The broad smile on her face fell when she saw the broken glass in the living room window frame.

"Mum, Mum!" I cried, dashing over to her. "It's Dad! I mean, it's Mr Lugs! Well, it's Dad *and* Mr Lugs!"

"Calm down, Lola. What are you talking about? What's happened?"

A sharp, sudden cry from somewhere along the street stopped me before I could properly start. "Help!" shouted a voice that sounded like Dad's. "Help me!"

"Was that your father?" asked Mum, as Scraps started to bark loudly.

I opened my mouth to tell her everything, when a rumble shook the ground beneath my feet. I watched in horror as a round hole opened up beneath Mum's feet. She seemed to hang there for a moment, like a character in a cartoon, then she dropped down into the darkness without a sound.

"Oh no, oh no, this is terrible!" yelped Harvey, running over to join me. "I just realized I forgot to save my game! I should go back in and– Hey, where did Mum go?"

Hand shaking, I pointed down into the hole. Scraps stood at the edge of it, sniffing the darkness and whimpering softly.

In the distance, I heard my dad's voice again – further away this time. "Help! Heeeeelp!"

"What do we do?" asked Harvey, hopping from foot to foot in panic. "What do we do?"

Chapter 5

We're Going on a Bunny Hunt

I stared into the hole, then off in the direction of Dad's cries for help. Normally, I don't mind making decisions – I'm quite good at it, in fact – but this was the biggest decision I'd ever been faced with in my life.

Mum or Dad? Who did we go after? If I didn't decide soon, it could be too late to help either of them. Harvey was useless, of course. It was all down to me.

"We go after Mum," I said. "That's what Dad would want us to do."

Harvey stared at me, his eyes wide. "Go down… *there?*" he said, pointing to the round hole in the road. "Us. Me and you. Go down *there?*"

"Come on," I urged, sitting down and dangling my legs into the darkness. "It'll be just like going into a cave in Minecraft."

"That's what I'm afraid of!" Harvey yelped. "Caves in Minecraft are full of giant spiders and skeletons with bows and arrows and –"

"*Get in this hole right now!*" I snapped, so fiercely I actually almost scared myself. Quick as a flash, Harvey sat down across from me. "OK," I said, "It'll be fine. I'll go first, you follow me. Scraps…."

I turned to the dog, but he was halfway to the house, running as fast as his legs would carry him. "Thanks a lot, you coward!" I cried. Scraps tucked his tail between his legs, but kept running. Harvey and I were on our own.

"Are you ready?" I asked.

Harvey stared at me. "Am I ready to climb down a tunnel to hunt for the giant mutant bunny rabbit who has kidnapped our mum?"

"Yep," I replied.

"Ready as I'll ever be… I guess," said Harvey.

"Great," I mumbled, pushing off with my arms and dropping down into the dark, dusty hole.

For some reason, I didn't think the hole would be very deep. I expected a drop of a couple of metres, then maybe a tunnel leading off to the right or left.

Instead, I kept falling. One second, two seconds, three seconds. The tunnel wall whipped upwards past me in the gloom.

Four seconds. Five seconds.

I heard a scream from somewhere right beside me. I twisted my head, searching for the source of the sound, then realized it was coming from my own mouth.

What were we on now? Nine seconds? Ten? I'd lost count. The light from the world above had faded and I was now falling through absolute darkness, plunging straight down. If Harvey and I hit the bottom at this speed we'd splatter like eggs, but there was no way of slowing, let alone stopping.

"*Get in the hole*, you said!" Harvey shrieked from somewhere just above me. "*It'll be fine*, you said!"

He was right. This was my fault. The decision had been down to me, and I had made the wrong call. How could I have been so–

BUMPSHHHHH!

The tunnel curved gently beneath me, so I was no longer falling, but sliding on softly packed soil instead. I realized I was still screaming, so I decided to stop. It wasn't really helping much.

I continued to hurtle downwards, but I could feel the ground gradually becoming more level. I was slowing down! After a few more seconds, I skidded to a stop at the bottom of the slope.

Moments later, Harvey landed on top of me.

"Argh! Who's that? *What's* that?" he yelped, slapping wildly at me with both hands.

"It's me, you clown," I growled. "You're sitting on my head!"

Harvey rolled off me. "I knew that," he said, trying to sound cool. I reached out to give him a jab, but missed him in the dark.

A light breeze tickled at the back of my neck. I turned towards it and felt the ground in front of me. The tunnel continued off in a straight line. There was no way we could climb back up, so we had no choice but to press on.

There was a faint *click,* then a light shone in my eyes, dazzling me.

"Ow! What are you doing?" I yelped. "I can't see, cut it out!"

Harvey moved the light away and I caught a flash of his broad grin. "Batman torch," he said, waving a little Caped-Crusader-shaped keyring around. The light shone from a bulb on the bottom of one of the superhero's feet. "Never leave home without it!"

Harvey swept the light across the walls. The tunnel was almost perfectly round. Tree roots snaked through the hard-packed soil, and worms wriggled from the ceiling above us.

"Come on, this way," I urged. My voice echoed strangely in the narrow passageway. I began to crawl in the direction of the breeze. "Stay close."

Harvey scurried forwards and jammed himself in between me and the tunnel wall. "I didn't mean that close," I said,

but he just gave a nervous giggle and
I didn't have the heart to tell him to
back off. Besides, if I'm honest having
him right there beside me helped make
me a little less scared.

We plodded on for a while in silence.
The tunnel floor curved upwards and
downwards, so sometimes we were
climbing and other times we were
slipping and sliding on our hands
and knees, out of control.

"We've been going for ages,"
moaned Harvey.

"You said that a minute ago," I replied
through gritted teeth.

"Are we nearly there yet?"

"How should I know? It's not like
I have a map is it?"

The torchlight flickered, casting

spooky shadows along the tunnel ahead of us.

"Uh-oh," said Harvey.

The light died away completely, and we were plunged into complete darkness once more.

"What happened?" I asked

Silence.

"Harvey?"

More silence.

The hairs on the back of my arm tingled. Something about the darkness was different.

"Harvey, stop being silly."

No answer.

Slowly, cautiously, I reached out into the darkness towards where Harvey should have been. My fingers found only empty space.

I felt the breeze again, but it wasn't coming from in front of me this time. It was coming from above. There was a smell to it, too. A smell that sent a shiver of fear all the way down my spine.

It was a smell like Mr Lugs's hutch when the teacher forgot to clean it.

Looking up, I saw a brief flash of white in the darkness. The last thing I felt before I fell unconscious was a strong furry fist wrapping around my throat and pulling me up into the gloom.

Chapter 6

Prisoners!

"Aaaargh! Skeleton!"

My eyes flickered open, but the bright light ahead almost forced them closed again. I could just make out Harvey sitting on the floor across from me. He was pointing, his hand trembling in fear.

"Skeleton!" he shouted again. "I told you this would happen. I told you!"

I tried to get my bearings. I was sitting on a solid floor, slumped against a wall. Sure enough, there was a human skeleton standing just three metres away, its empty eye sockets staring straight at us.

Unlike Harvey, I wasn't worried. I recognized the skeleton straight away. After all, I was the one who'd built it.

"It's fake," I said. "It's the one I helped make for the school play. But I thought that was in…" I looked around at the small room we were in. I recognized that quickly, too. "…the school basement."

The light that was shining in my face was from the stage lighting rig that was kept down here in the cellar when it wasn't in use. Only one of the smaller lights was on, thankfully. Had it been the main spotlight I wouldn't have been able to see a thing.

"This is the school basement?" asked Harvey. "Why are we here?"

"Because I wanted you here," said a voice from somewhere behind the light. It was a soft, raspy voice that came like a whisper from the darkness. "But I shouldn't start a sentence with 'because'," it muttered. "Or with 'but'. Wrong, wrong, must try harder. Bottom of the class, bottom of the class."

I peered into the shadows. It wasn't easy, but I could just make out a figure standing there, holding his arms straight up above his head.

Wait… those weren't arms.

"M-Mr Lugs?" I stammered.

With a single springing leap he appeared in front of us. I gasped, unable to believe what I was seeing. Everything about him was… no, not just big. I mean, yes, he was big, but he was different, too. He no longer looked like a rabbit, more like a man wearing a rabbit costume. He was what I'd imagine the Easter Bunny would look like. The Easter Bunny having the worst day of his entire life, that is.

His paws were caked with mud, only they weren't paws any more, they were more like hands. Huge hands the size of shovels, with three fingers and a thumb on each. The fingers fidgeted as he shuffled closer and closer towards me.

"Good girl, clever girl, top of the class," he said, his whiskers trembling with every word. "Clever, like Mr Lugs clever. But Mr Lugs is not clever enough… not yet."

He lifted one of his hands to his mouth and I realized he wasn't fidgeting with his fingers, he was toying with one of my dad's rare plants. His two front teeth snipped the head from the flower's stalk and he hurriedly swallowed it down.

A shudder travelled the length of his body and he seemed to grow another few centimetres before my eyes. "Brain power boosting," he said, and a gleeful grin spread across his face. "Intelligence levels getting higher.…"

With a final twitch, Mr Lugs stood sharply to attention. He looked down at the remains of the flower and raised one eyebrow. "Fascinating," he said. Then he tossed the flower stem into the corner.

"Hang on… is that Mr Lugs?" Harvey asked.

The rabbit-man rolled his eyes and sighed. "Oh Harvey, you never were the sharpest knife in the drawer, but do try to keep up. Yes, I'm Mr Lugs, yes I'm a super-intelligent mutant mega-bunny, and yes, I led you here on purpose."

Mr Lugs glanced back towards the steps that led up into the main school building. A wicked glint flashed in his eyes. "Would you like to see why?"

Chapter 7

Rise Rabbits, Rise

I glanced across at Harvey. If I could get his attention we could work together to attack Mr Lugs. But no, Harvey was too busy staring at the giant rabbit to notice me waggling my eyebrows at him. I sighed. As sidekicks went, Harvey was pretty much the worst.

I turned my gaze to Mr Lugs. That last bite of exotic plant was really having an effect on him. He had already been standing on two feet, but he had been hunched over, and his movements had been awkward and uncertain.

Now, though, his shoulders were back and his head was held high. He peered down at me as if I were little more than a bug – a bug he could squash at any moment.

"Time's ticking. Tick-tock, tick-tock," he said. "What is your answer? Would you like to see my reason for bringing you here?"

His tongue flicked out and licked across his sharp front teeth. His eyes went to my feet. "Or would you prefer me to give you both a really nasty nibble? The choice is yours."

Harvey's hand shot up. "First one," he said. "Definitely the first one."

Mr Lugs ignored him. He'd obviously figured out that I was the brains of the outfit. I stood up, very slowly and deliberately, trying to look as if I wasn't more scared than I'd ever been in my life.

"No harm in taking a look, I suppose," I said.

A flash of wickedness passed behind Mr Lugs's dark eyes. "Oh," he smirked. "I wouldn't say that."

Stepping aside, the man-rabbit gestured towards the stairs that led up into the school. "Now, if you'd care to hop this way, I'm afraid that time is against us."

Harvey was still sitting down. He seemed dazed, as if fear had slowed his brain down to a crawl. I caught him by the back of his sweatshirt and pulled him to his feet. He didn't resist as I marched him over to the bottom step.

"Don't worry, we're going to be fine," I whispered. "We'll get out of this."

Somehow, I added in my head.

"Where's our mum and dad?" I asked as Mr Lugs urged us up the first few steps. "What have you done with them?"

"All in good time," said Mr Lugs, and there was something about the way he said it that made a shudder of dread pass through me from head to toe. "For now, climb."

In silence, Harvey and I made our way to the top of the stairs. I was just about to push open the door that led out into the school when someone pulled it from the other side. Off-balance, I staggered through the door and into the corridor, only to be caught by something that was 50 per cent hand, 50 per cent paw and 100 per cent creepy. It was another mutant bunny!

"Hoooman," it growled. Shorter than me, and less than half the size of Mr Lugs, its squat, stocky body was made up of densely packed muscle. Its nose was flat and wide. As it snuffled in close to me I tried to pull away, but its grip on my arm was too tight.

"Taaasty hoooman," the rabbit creature muttered. "Yummmmy hoooman."

"Let go," I yelped, trying to yank my arm free. The bunny-thing's whiskers trembled with excitement. "Let go, you're hurting me!"

"Hey! Leave my sister alone."

The tone of Harvey's voice took me by surprise. He stepped forward and grabbed the muscle-bound bunny by the wrist. For a moment, I thought it was going to bite his arm off, but then Mr Lugs appeared in the doorway behind us.

"Let the girl go, Grunt," he said. He didn't shout, but his tone made the other rabbit take a hop back in fright.

"Yessss, masssster," Grunt whimpered. With a final hungry glance at me, he turned and bounded off along the corridor in the direction of the school canteen.

"Forgive him," Mr Lugs said. "He is young and wild. He knows no better. Now, kindly follow me."

He hopped off in the opposite direction to the other bunny, keeping a close eye on us to make sure we were following. It felt strange being in school when everyone else had gone home. All the familiar noises that brought the place alive during the day had fallen silent, and the only sound was the *thudding* of Mr Lugs's huge feet on the floor.

"Thanks, Harvey," I whispered.

Harvey frowned. "What for?"

"For standing up to that other rabbit."

"Come on. Nobody pushes my sister around," Harvey said. He smiled, but I could tell he was faking it. He was just as terrified as I was.

"Where did he come from – Grunt, I mean?" I asked. My voice echoed along the corridor ahead of us.

"I discovered him lurking beneath a hedge on the way here and decided to feed him one of your father's wonderful plants," Mr Lugs explained. "I wanted to be sure its effect would work on others of my species, too."

"And did it?" Harvey asked.

I rolled my eyes. "Of course it did, Harvey. You just met the result."

"Oh, yeah," said Harvey. "Good point."

Mr Lugs stopped at a classroom door. It wasn't just any classroom, either. It was my classroom, the one where Harvey and I had been given Mr Lugs to look after just a few short hours earlier.

The brass doorknob crumpled in Mr Lugs's grip. "Oops," he said, letting the door swing open. "Don't know my own strength."

Lowering his ears and ducking his head, he led us into the classroom.

For a moment, I thought about running away, but he'd catch us easily. If he didn't then there was the chance of bumping into Grunt, and that scared me even more. I could tell there was something wicked about Mr Lugs, though he didn't seem to want to hurt us.

Not yet, anyway.

Chapter 8

The Plan Revealed

I stepped into the classroom and immediately spotted the whiteboard. It was covered in numbers and diagrams. They started off as childish scribbles on the left, but slowly became more complicated as the writing got nearer the middle of the board.

Mr Lugs hopped to the head of the class and picked up a marker pen. He began to scrawl furiously, the pen squeaking as it danced and flowed across the board.

"Add that.... Adjust for wind-speed.... Divide by the force of gravity...."

I studied the scribbles, but they had turned into one long and difficult equation, and I had no idea what any of it meant. "What's he doing?" I wondered.

"Writing stuff," said Harvey, as if that explained everything.

"Yes, well I can see that," I sighed. "I meant what does it all mean?"

Mr Lugs spun on the spot. "Isn't it obvious?" he asked. "I am working out something *amazing*."

He began to shuffle towards us. "You see, for years I have sat in this classroom, listening to teacher after teacher go over the same old facts and figures time and time again. On and on, blah-de-blah-de-blah," he said.

His nose crinkled up in what looked like disgust. "Do you know the worst thing about you humans? You're boring. You have no imagination. You sit there and learn about old battles and old languages and what the world used to be like."

A demented grin of glee crept across his face. "It no longer matters what the world used to be like. As of today, I'm going to change it forever. And I'd like you to help, Lola."

I glanced sideways at Harvey. "Me? Why me?"

"You saved me," Mr Lugs said. "When your father threw me across the room, you leapt to my aid and caught me. As a token of gratitude, I am offering you the chance to rule by my side."

"Rule what?" asked Harvey.

"Everything," said Mr Lugs in a voice that sounded like a giggle. "All those squiggles and signs on the board are a genius scientific calculation I have carried out."

"Calculation of what?" I asked, nervously.

"That's the clever bit," Mr Lugs went on. "I have worked out how to spread the pollen from your dad's wonderful plants all over the country, thus bringing about the rise of a rabbit empire that will obey my every word."

I shook my head in disbelief. "You must be joking."

Mr Lugs's expression turned icy cold. "Do I look as if I'm joking? Don't you get it? There are 45 million wild rabbits in this country, and all those… how shall I put it… 'pet' rabbits, too. And we can have up to 16 babies every month. You do the maths. We'll outnumber you by Christmas. The human race's reign is over. It's time to give another species a chance. But first…."

There was a commotion from over by the door. I looked across in time to see a large box with a sheet over it being wheeled into the classroom by Grunt. Mr Lugs was beside it with one quick hop. He grinned as he pulled the sheet aside to reveal….

"Mum! Dad!" Harvey shouted. "You're alive!"

They groaned. They were alive, but they both looked only semi-conscious. They were wedged tightly into a small cage. Even if they had been fully awake, there would have been nothing they could do to help us. Harvey and I were on our own.

Mr Lugs loomed over us. He seemed impossibly tall, as if he was still getting bigger with every minute that passed.

"My offer is this," he said. "Join me and rule by my side, or be caged up along with the rest of the human race and fed nothing but carrots and lettuce for the rest of your lives. Let's see how you like it!"

That glint of wickedness blazed across his face once more. "So, Lola," he grinned. "What's it to be?"

Chapter 9

Surprise, Surprise!

"So let me get this straight," I said. "You want me to help you stick humans in cages?"

Mr Lugs nodded excitedly, making his ears flap about. "All humans, yes."

"And force-feed them salad vegetables?"

Mr Lugs nodded again. "Correct!"

"And in return I'll get to rule the world alongside you?"

"Well, technically I'll be the one doing the actual world ruling, but I'll let you watch."

I squared my shoulders and tried to stand nose-to-nose with the big bunny-beast. As he was now much taller than I was, it didn't really work, and I ended up sort of nose-to-belly instead.

"No."

Mr Lugs's face darkened. "I beg your pardon?"

I glanced over at Harvey, who was anxiously rocking from foot to foot. Behind him, the muscle-bound mutant rabbit, Grunt, was staring hungrily at my parents trapped inside the little cage.

And over on the teacher's desk were the things that had caused all this – the exotic plants Mr Lugs had first nibbled on back in Dad's greenhouse. There were dozens of the flower buds left –

67

more than enough for Mr Lugs to put his world domination plan into action.

"I'm not going to help you. If you want to take over the world…" I took a deep breath, "…you'll have to get through me, first."

"Through b-both of us," stammered Harvey, stepping forward to join me. I held his hand and squeezed it tightly.

Mr Lugs stared at us both for a moment, then shrugged. "Fair enough," he said. He raised his huge furry fists above his head and roared as he swung them down towards us. Harvey and I leaped in different directions, narrowly avoiding being flattened.

From somewhere by the door there came a sharp sudden *BARK!* A bundle of black fur came bounding into the classroom, snarling and snapping and baring its teeth.

"Scraps!" I cried, as our dog hurled itself at Mr Lugs, jaws open wide.

Before Scraps could sink his teeth in, though, he gave a short, sudden yelp of pain. Grunt had caught him by the tail in one powerful paw-like hand. The bunny grinned as he spun Scraps around on the spot then launched him across the classroom.

With a loud *SMASH*, Scraps crashed through the teacher's desk. He flipped awkwardly over the back of the desk, slammed against the whiteboard, then dropped to the floor.

I held my breath and realized Harvey was doing the same. Scraps lay on the floor, not moving. The teacher's paperwork, pens and bits of exotic plant lay scattered around him.

"You killed Scraps," Harvey yelped. His fingers curled into tight fists. "You killed our dog!"

Howling with rage, Harvey flew at Grunt, fists flying furiously. The brown-furred bunny smirked as he batted the attacks away and caught my brother in a vice-like grip.

"Get off me! Let me go!" Harvey yelped.

"Tasty hooman," smirked Grunt. "Grunt hungry for tasty hooman."

"Leave him alone!" I cried. I tried to reach for Harvey, but Mr Lugs caught me by the arm and dragged me back.

"This could all have been avoided, Lola," said the white-furred monster.

"You could have worked with us, but I'm afraid you leave us no choice."

Mr Lugs's gums drew back, revealing his huge, sharp teeth. I squirmed and wriggled, trying to get free, but his grip on my arm was too tight. I shut my eyes as his mouth opened.

Chapter 10

Big Bully Bunny

"Let my family go."

The voice was gruff and gravelly and came from over by the whiteboard. I opened my eyes and gasped in shock. There, standing on the teacher's desk, was Scraps!

I glanced down at the floor where the flowers had fallen. They were all gone. Scraps had eaten every last petal, and he was now growing at an amazing rate.

He looked as if he'd been crossed with a lion. His body was three times bigger than normal, and his skinny legs were now thick, with bulging muscles. Scraps leapt down from the desk and the floor shook as he landed.

"The flowers!" shrieked Mr Lugs. "You've eaten all my wonderful flowers!"

"Yeah," I said. "Scraps will eat pretty much anything."

Swinging back my leg I kicked Mr Lugs in the shins. He hissed in pain and grabbed at his leg, letting me twist free.

"Harvey, the whiskers!" I shouted. Harvey blinked, confused, then understood my meaning. Reaching up, he grabbed Grunt's whiskers in both hands and yanked sharply outwards.

Grunt's squeal shook the windows in their frame. He tried to leap away, but Harvey hung on tight. There was a series of *twangs*, like the strings of a guitar snapping, and Grunt stumbled into Mum and Dad's cage, completely whisker-less.

Mr Lugs made another grab for me, but Scraps bounded on to his back. They spun around and around, smashing through desks and ripping children's paintings from the walls as Mr Lugs tried to tear Scraps off him.

"Scraps!" I cried. The dog was big, but Mr Lugs was still much bigger. Grunt was getting back to his feet now, too, and he *really* didn't look happy.

"Go," barked Scraps. "Get out of here. Take Mum and Dad."

"But–"

"*Go!*"

Mr Lugs threw himself backwards, slamming Scraps against the wall so hard the plaster cracked in a wide spider-web pattern.

I ran over to the cage with my parents wedged inside. It was on wheels, but even though I pushed with all my strength I couldn't get it to budge. I gritted my teeth and dug down deep. I had to get Mum and Dad out of there. I *had* to!

Harvey appeared beside me and put his shoulder against the cage. "Push together," he said. "We can do this!"

Straining and struggling, we finally got the cage to move. Slowly, steadily, it began to pick up speed as we steered it towards the exit.

We were almost at the door when a large shadow passed above us. I looked back to see Grunt bounding towards us, his face twisted into a snarl. There was nothing I could do – no way to escape. He was right on us. We were done for!

Then – *crunch* – Scraps slammed into Grunt, sending him spinning across the classroom. I watched on in amazement. A moment ago, Scraps had been the size of a lion. Now he was the size of a giant grizzly bear!

"Come on, sis!" urged Harvey. I ducked my head and we heaved the hutch out into the corridor. The wheels squeaked as we hurried in the direction of the fire exit. If we could only reach it, we could get outside. And if we could get outside we'd be safe!

At least, I hoped we would.

"LOLA!"

There was a splintering crash from behind us as the classroom door was kicked clean off its hinges. I turned to see Mr Lugs come stumbling into the corridor, his face fixed in an expression of pure fury.

"Go, go, hurry!" I yelped, helping Harvey shove the cage the last few metres to the fire exit. Pushing down the bar I threw open the door and we wrestled the human-hutch out into the cool evening air.

"Get to safety," I said.

Harvey frowned. "What? What about you?"

"I'll keep him busy," I said, and before Harvey could answer I stepped back into the school and pulled the door closed.

Mr Lugs stood just along the corridor. His ears twitched with rage and his paw hands were bunched into fists. I could hear Scraps and Grunt still locked in battle. There would be nobody leaping to my defence this time.

"You ruined my plan," Mr Lugs growled. He took a hop towards me. I thought about running, but I knew he'd catch me in seconds. Besides, I didn't want to run any more. Instead, I started to walk towards him.

Mr Lugs hesitated. He hadn't been expecting that. "What are you doing?" he demanded.

"What I should have done down in the basement," I said. I kept walking until I was standing right in front of him, then I folded my arms and fixed him with my most icy stare. "You are a bully," I told him. "And I don't let bullies push me around."

Mr Lugs blinked. "What?"

"You heard," I said. "You told us you'd been listening in class. Didn't you pay attention to the lessons on bullying? Don't you know that threatening people is *not* acceptable?"

"What? But I… I mean…."

"Every kid in this school loved you, Mr Lugs," I continued. "And how do you repay them? By making a plan to lock them up in cages and stuff them full of vegetables. It's not on."

Mr Lugs looked confused. His nose twitched. He nibbled nervously at his bottom lip. His wide eyes darted left and right. "That's… I didn't…."

With a growl, Mr Lugs gave himself a shake. "No," he snapped. "I won't let you trick me!" He bent down so his face was right next to mine. "I'm the future king of the world."

"No," I said. I flicked him on the end of his nose. "You're a very naughty bunny."

Mr Lugs sprang back in shock, covering his nose with his paws. As I watched, his ears grew stubbier and his broad shoulders became more slender. He was shrinking. Mr Lugs was shrinking before my eyes!

"What's happening?" he yelped, getting smaller with every moment that passed.

"It's wearing off," I said, laughing with relief. "The flowers are wearing off!"

"Noooo!" Mr Lugs wailed. "I'll get you for this. I'll get you for–"

The last word came out as a soft nibbly noise. With a faint *pop*, Mr Lugs returned to rabbit size and landed in the middle of the floor. He hopped over to me, sniffed my left foot, then did a tiny rabbity-poo on my shoe.

There was a commotion further along the corridor. Scraps strolled out of the classroom, now walking on his back legs. He was so huge he had to duck his head to avoid hitting it on the ceiling.

In one hand, Scraps carried the wriggling Grunt. He, too, had started to shrink, and before I knew it, he was a frightened little wild rabbit once more.

Scraps dropped Grunt, and the bunny tore off along the corridor and vanished into the school. Wagging his tail, Scraps paced over to my side.

"Some day, huh?" he said.

I nodded. "You can say that again."

Scraps scratched his head. "Want to go throw a stick or something?"

I smiled. Some things never changed. "Sounds like fun," I said, picking Mr Lugs up and tucking him under my arm. I took Scraps by the paw and together we headed for the school's main door, and the big wide world that lay beyond.

THE END

FICTION EXPRESS

THE READERS TAKE CONTROL!

Have you ever wanted to change the course of a plot, change a character's destiny, tell an author what to write next?

Well, now you can!

'Rise of the Rabbits' was originally written for the award-winning interactive e-book website Fiction Express.

Fiction Express e-books are published in gripping weekly episodes. At the end of each episode, readers are given voting options to decide where the plot goes next. They vote online and the winning vote is then conveyed to the author who writes the next episode, in real time, according to the readers' most popular choice.

www.fictionexpress.co.uk

WINNER
Education Resources
Award for Innovation

FICTI●N EXPRESS

TALK TO THE AUTHORS

The Fiction Express website features a blog where readers can interact with the authors while they are writing. An exciting and unique opportunity!

FANTASTIC TEACHER RESOURCES

Each weekly Fiction Express episode comes with a PDF of teacher resources packed with ideas to extend the text.

"The teaching resources are fab and easily fill a whole week of literacy lessons!"
Rachel Humphries, teacher at Westacre Middle School

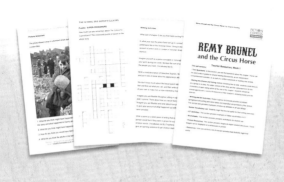

FICTI😊N EXPRESS

Rémy Brunel and the Circus Horse
by Sharon Gosling

"Roll up, roll up, and see the greatest show on Earth!" Rémy Brunel loves her life in the circus – riding elephants, practising tightrope tricks and dazzling audiences. But when two new magicians arrive at the circus, everyone is wary of them. What exactly are they up to? What secrets are they trying to hide? Should Rémy and her new friend Matthias trust them?

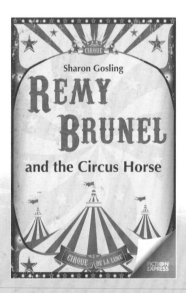

ISBN 978-1-783-22469-2

FICTI●N EXPRESS

The Time Detectives:
The Mystery of Maddie Musgrove
by Alex Woolf

When Joe Smallwood goes to stay with his Uncle Theo and cousin Maya life seems dull, until he finds a strange smartphone nestling beside a gravestone. The phone enables Joe and Maya to become time-travelling detectives and takes them on an exciting adventure back to Victorian times. Can they prove maidservant Maddie Musgrove's innocence? Can they save her from the gallows?

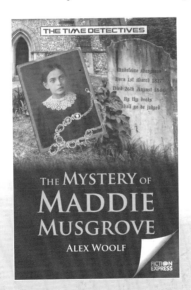

ISBN 978-1-783-22459-3

About the Author

Barry Hutchison was born and raised in the Highlands of Scotland. Despite this, he has never once tossed a caber, wrestled a haggis, or gone a-roamin' in the gloamin'.

An avid reader from a very early age, Barry spent most of his childhood with his nose buried in some book or another, and began writing his own novels when he was 10. His first epic – the mind-blowingly violent *Nightwarrior vs The Death Ninjas* – has mercifully long since been lost to the mists of time.

Barry still lives in the Highlands, where he spends his days writing, eating and hiding from his two children. His biggest fear is that someone will some day discover how much fun his job is and immediately put a stop to it. His second biggest fear is squirrels.